D

# Lucy's
# Tricks and Treats

# Lucy's Tricks and Treats

by Ilene Cooper

illustrated by David Merrell

A STEPPING STONE BOOK™

Random House 🏠 New York

To all the girls and boys who love Lucy as much as I do.
And thank you to Kay Weisman for reading the manuscript and
giving me valuable input on hearing disabilities.
—I.C.

For Mason, Sophia, Matthew, and Ethan
—D.M.

Text copyright © 2012 by Ilene Cooper
Interior illustrations copyright © 2012 by David Merrell
Cover illustration copyright © 2012 by Mary Ann Lasher

All rights reserved. Published in the United States by Random House
Children's Books, a division of Random House, Inc., New York.

Random House and the colophon are registered trademarks and A Stepping Stone
Book and the colophon are trademarks of Random House, Inc.

Visit us on the Web!
SteppingStonesBooks.com
randomhouse.com/kids

Educators and librarians, for a variety of teaching tools, visit us at
RHTeachersLibrarians.com

Library of Congress Cataloging-in-Publication Data
Cooper, Ilene.
Lucy's tricks and treats / by Ilene Cooper ; illustrated by David Merrell.
p. cm. — (Absolutely Lucy ; 5)
"A Stepping Stone Book."
Summary: Halloween is near and Bobby has a great idea for costumes for himself
and his dog, Lucy, but when he brings Lucy's costume to school for show-and-tell it
disappears, and Bobby suspects the unfriendly new student took it.
ISBN 978-0-375-86997-6 (pbk.) — ISBN 978-0-375-96997-3 (lib. bdg.) —
ISBN 978-0-375-98637-6 (ebook)
[1. Halloween—Fiction. 2. Costume—Fiction. 3. Lost and found
possessions—Fiction. 4. Beagle (Dog breed)—Fiction. 5. Dogs—Fiction.
6. Schools—Fiction.] I. Merrell, David, ill. II. Title.
PZ7.C7856Lvt 2012   [E]—dc23   2011042084

Printed in the United States of America
10 9 8 7 6 5 4 3 2 1

# Contents

# Here Comes Halloween!

The leaves were turning colors—red, orange, yellow, and brown. The air was getting chilly. It was autumn for sure. That meant one thing to Bobby Quinn and his friends Shawn and Candy. Halloween!

"I'm going to be a pirate!" Bobby said as they walked home from school.

"I might be an astronaut," Shawn said. "What about you, Candy?"

"Well, I thought about being a fairy," Candy said. "Then I thought lots of the girls might be fairies. So maybe I'll be a queen. My mother has one of those sparkly crowns somewhere. But she probably won't be able to find it. A witch! A witch would be good. Don't forget we get to wear our costumes twice on Halloween. Trick-or-treating and at the school parade!"

Candy was a talker. Bobby and Shawn were shy. Not as shy as they used to be, though.

"Are you going to make your costume? Or are you going to buy it?" Shawn asked Bobby.

Bobby shrugged. He wasn't sure. But he had a reason for being a pirate. He didn't want to talk about it yet. If his idea worked out, it would make being a pirate extra-special. "I'm hoping there's going to be a pirate surprise" was all he would say.

The three kids stopped at Bobby's house. Shawn lived across the street. Candy's house was a few blocks away.

"Hey, Lucy's waiting for you," Shawn said, pointing at the Quinns' living-room window.

Lucy was Bobby's dog. She was a little brown-and-white beagle. She had a few black spots and chocolate-colored eyes.

Lucy *was* waiting for Bobby, but she wasn't waiting patiently.

She stood at the window with her paws on the glass. Small howls interrupted short barks. She wiggled around.

"Lucy's doing her happy dance," Candy said. "I wish Butch did a happy dance when I came home."

Bobby and Shawn looked at each other.

They tried not to laugh. Butch, Candy's dog, was maybe the laziest dog they had ever met. It was hard to picture him getting off the couch when Candy came home. A happy dance? Absolutely not!

Bobby said goodbye to his friends. He was barely inside the house when Lucy dashed over to him. She leapt into his arms. She licked his face. Bobby smiled. Lucy acted as if he had been gone for a month.

"Hey, girl," Bobby said, "calm down."

Lucy got the message. She wriggled to the floor. Then she looked up at him. She seemed to be saying, *Let's have some fun.*

"Okay, Lucy. Maybe we'll go for a walk," Bobby said.

*Walk!* Lucy knew that word.

Before Bobby could get Lucy's leash, his mother came into the hallway.

"Hi, Mom. I'm taking Lucy out," Bobby told her.

Mrs. Quinn smiled, but she looked tired. "That's a very good idea. Do you want to say hello to your father first?"

"Dad's home?" Bobby asked, surprised.

"He came home early," his mother answered. "We're getting started on the nursery."

Up until that day, the "nursery" had been Mr. Quinn's office. Now the Quinn family was waiting for the adoption agency to bring them a baby. Bobby's parents weren't sure when that would be. It could be tomorrow. It could be months from now. Mrs. Quinn wanted to be ready.

Thinking about the baby made Bobby feel funny. It had been just the three of them for eight years. Mom, Dad, and Bobby. Then Lucy had joined them last summer. She had changed everything for Bobby. He had been very shy. But Lucy was so friendly and so much fun. Everyone liked being around her. She helped him make lots of new friends.

Bobby hoped the baby would work out half as well as Lucy had.

"We need to keep Lucy out of the office," his mother said. "She wants to get in the middle of things."

Bobby nodded. If there was one place Lucy liked to be, it was in the middle of things. "I'll try," he said.

Mr. Quinn came into the hall. "Hi, Bobby," he said. He ruffled Bobby's hair.

"How's it going?" Bobby asked.

"Well, the desk is in the middle of the room, and the stuff from that closet is on the floor. But I guess we're making progress," Mr. Quinn said. He didn't look all that sure.

"Do you want to have a look?" Mrs. Quinn asked. "I can show you the new wallpaper. It's yellow with rainbows. Good for a boy or a girl."

"Oh, it's going to be a boy," Bobby said.

"Why do you think so?" his father asked.

"Because boys are more fun," Bobby replied promptly.

"Lucy is a girl," his mother pointed out.

Before Bobby could say, "But she's a dog," Mrs. Quinn turned to her husband. "You closed the office door, didn't you?"

Mr. Quinn made a face. "I think so."

A loud crash came from the office.

"Lucy!" everyone said together.

They hurried down the hallway to the office.

Mr. Quinn had not remembered to close the door.

The room didn't look like an office now. And it certainly didn't look like a nursery. It looked like a big mess.

The stuff from the closet was scattered across the floor. A cup of coffee had been knocked over. A small river of the dark liquid headed for the door. Next to the coffee cup, two half-chewed doughnuts lay on the paper bag Lucy had pulled them from.

Lucy had managed to do a lot in very little time.

"Where is she?" Mrs. Quinn asked.

Mr. Quinn pointed under the desk at a mounded white sheet.

At first Bobby was confused. But then the sheet started rustling. From under it came a spooky howl.

"Looks like Lucy wants to dress up for

Halloween, too," Mrs. Quinn said. "As a ghost."

Bobby kneeled by the desk and lifted the sheet. Lucy barely looked up when the sheet came off. Something was between her paws—a piece of yellow wallpaper dotted with rainbows. She was busy shredding it with her teeth.

"She had been doing so well," Mrs. Quinn said with a sigh.

"She's hardly caused any trouble in weeks," Bobby said, trying to defend his dog.

"You can't really blame her," Mr. Quinn said. "How could she help herself? A room like this, with stuff everywhere, must have looked like an amusement park to Lucy."

Bobby shook his head. "And she went on all the rides."

## 2

# Yo Ho Ho!

"Lucy's in the doghouse," Mr. Quinn told Bobby.

"We don't have a doghouse," Bobby said.

"It's just a saying," Mr. Quinn replied. "It means Lucy's in trouble. I'm in the doghouse, too," he added. "Your mom kept reminding me to keep the office door closed."

The night before, Bobby's mother hadn't said much during dinner. Then she told them she had a headache and went to bed early.

Now, late on Saturday morning, she was still asleep.

"Let's do something nice for Mom," Mr. Quinn said.

"What?" Bobby asked.

"We'll do the Saturday errands, so she can relax," he answered.

"Can we take Lucy with us?" Bobby wanted to know.

Lucy heard her name. She came bounding into the living room, where Bobby and his father were sitting. She didn't seem to know she was in the doghouse.

"Oh, definitely," Mr. Quinn said. He looked around for Lucy's leash. "I think your mother would be disappointed if we didn't."

Bobby and his dad got in the car. Lucy got in the backseat. She started making soft little growling noises. Bobby and his father knew that meant *Open the window!*

"Hold on, Lucy," Mr. Quinn said. "I have to start the car."

"Where are we going first?" Bobby asked once they were on their way.

His father reached into the pocket of his jean jacket and pulled out a crumpled piece of paper. "Here's the list."

Bobby unfolded it. "Bank," he read, "library, and Pet-O-Rama."

*Great!* he thought. Pet-O-Rama was where his surprise was.

They parked in front of the bank and got out of the car. Mr. Quinn said, "Bobby, you'll have to stay outside with Lucy. Don't go too far."

Mr. Quinn had just gone into the bank when Lucy noticed someone coming out.

Lucy tugged at her leash. It was someone she knew.

Their neighbor Mr. Davis was walking slowly out of the bank.

"Hello, Bobby. Hello, Lucy." Mr. Davis lifted his cane a bit off the sidewalk and waved it at them.

"Hi, Mr. D.," Bobby answered. Even though Mr. Davis was old, older than Bobby's grandparents, Bobby liked talking to him. He had interesting stories to tell.

"Have a moment to sit, Bobby?" asked Mr. Davis. He pointed to a nearby bench.

"Sure," Bobby said, joining him. "I'm waiting for my dad."

Lucy could be wild sometimes, but she seemed to know that she had to be calm with Mr. Davis. She jumped on the bench and put her head on his knee.

"So, Bobby," Mr. Davis said, "Hallow-een's right around the corner. Do you know what you're going to be?"

Bobby nodded. "Yep. A pirate."

Mr. Davis patted Lucy's head. "A pirate, huh? Say, I have a black patch from when I had eye problems a while back. Would you like to borrow it for your costume?"

"An eye patch would be perfect," Bobby said. He would look like a real pirate!

"Well, it's all yours." Mr. Davis nodded. "Have you ever heard of the book *Treasure Island*?"

Bobby shook his head.

"It's about a fierce pirate, a fellow named Long John Silver," Mr. Davis told him. "And Jim, the ship's cabin boy. Not much older than you. There's a dangerous search for a hidden treasure. . . ."

Mr. Quinn came up to them. "Hi, Mr. Davis. What are you guys talking about?" he asked.

Mr. Davis smiled. "I was about to ask Bobby if he wanted to borrow my copy of *Treasure Island*."

Mr. Quinn smiled. "Bobby and I can read it together. I loved that book when I was a boy."

"I'll come by to pick it up," Bobby said, getting up from the bench, with Lucy right behind him. "And the eye patch!"

"They'll be waiting for you, Bobby," Mr. Davis said with a smile.

Next, Bobby and his father took a quick trip to the library. They weren't going in today, just returning books in the metal book drop. Lucy gave a small yip each time a book went down the chute.

Then it was time for Pet-O-Rama. Now Bobby was getting excited.

Lucy was getting excited, too. She loved Pet-O-Rama! Maybe it was because it had all her favorite treats. Maybe it was because it was one of the few stores where dogs were welcome. Or maybe it was because Lucy had happy memories of being in a pet contest there. Whatever it was, Lucy always seemed to know they were heading toward Pet-O-Rama before the parking lot even came into sight.

Her nose started quivering, and her ears pressed flat against her head. And although Lucy couldn't exactly smile, the look on her face might have been taken for a grin.

"What are we buying here?" Bobby asked as they all got out of the car. He knew what he *hoped* they'd be buying, but he didn't want to tell his dad about it—he wanted to show him.

"Mom forgot the chewy bones Lucy likes so much when you were here the other day." Mr. Quinn snapped Lucy's leash on her collar. "When Lucy doesn't have her chewy bones . . ."

Mr. Quinn didn't have to finish. When Lucy didn't have her chewy bones, she found plenty of other things to chew.

Inside, a wide aisle divided the brightly lit store in two. On one side were mostly pet supplies. On the other side were the animals you could buy—turtles, birds, fish. Shawn had bought his mouse, Twitch, here.

Lucy was definitely interested in looking at the animals. She tugged on her leash. She wanted to watch the parakeets fluttering around in their big glass cage.

"Not today, Lucy," Mr. Quinn said. "We'll just pick up the chewy bones and then go." He looked around. Pet-O-Rama was large and filled with many things to buy. "Do you know where those bones are, Bobby?"

Now was the moment Bobby had been waiting for.

"Sure, Dad," Bobby said. "But can I show you something first? It's right over here."

Before Mr. Quinn could answer, Bobby led his father and Lucy to a rack of Halloween items. Catnip treats in the shapes of witches and ghosts sat next to dog bones striped black and orange. Behind them was a whole rack of costumes for pets. A dog or cat could be anything from a bee to a zebra.

Bobby riffled through the rack. There it was! "Dad, look, a pet pirate costume. See, isn't it great?"

A small black-and-white-striped T-shirt and a plastic bag with four tiny black boots were on a hanger. The best part of the costume was pinned to the T-shirt—a black pirate hat painted with a white skull and crossbones!

"Let me get this straight," Mr. Quinn said. "You think Lucy will let you dress her in a pirate costume?"

Bobby hadn't thought about whether Lucy would wear the costume. He had just thought about how good she would look in it.

Mr. Quinn shook his head. "Lucy is way too squirmy."

"But, Dad . . ."

"I admit, this costume is neat," Mr. Quinn said. He took it out of Bobby's hands and looked it over.

Bobby felt hopeful. His father liked the

outfit. "See, I thought we could both be pirates," Bobby explained.

"I just don't think she'd wear it," Mr. Quinn said, handing the costume back to Bobby.

Bobby didn't know what he could do to change his father's mind.

Lucy had been sitting quietly on her haunches. Now she gave a sharp bark.

Both Bobby and Mr. Quinn turned to look at Lucy. Her nose was quivering. Her tail was, too.

Bobby held the costume next to Lucy's face. He hoped she wouldn't start to chew it.

Lucy did not chew it. She did sniff it. She sniffed the little striped shirt, and she sniffed the pirate hat. She licked the bag with the boots.

"Do you like it, Lucy?" Bobby asked.

Did she ever! She closed her eyes and rubbed her cheek against the shirt. It looked as if the costume was making Lucy very happy indeed.

"Dad, can we get it?" Bobby asked.

"All right," Mr. Quinn said with a sigh. "We'll give it a try. Captain Lucy, the most dangerous pirate on the seven seas."

Lucy opened one eye. *"Arf."*

# Pumpkins
# for Dragons

**"S**he'll never wear it." That was the first thing Mrs. Quinn said when she saw Lucy's pirate costume.

"She seems to like it," Mr. Quinn said.

"It smells good to her," Bobby added helpfully.

Mrs. Quinn shrugged. "Well, I suppose we can try to put it on."

Lucy was staring at the pirate costume.

She seemed to be smelling it, too. Her nose was twitching.

Bobby brought the costume closer. Lucy's tail wagged hard. She gave an excited bark.

"Okay, I see what you mean." Mrs. Quinn laughed. "But that doesn't mean she'll actually wear it."

Bobby thought that might be true. To the surprise of all of them, though, Lucy couldn't wait to put it on.

Bobby slipped the striped shirt over her head. She hardly wriggled at all.

He put the pirate hat on her head, and Lucy gave a happy howl.

She looked confused when Bobby put the little black boots on her paws, but she didn't try to get them off.

"Let me take a picture of this," Mr. Quinn said, whipping his phone out of his pocket.

"She looks adorable," Mrs. Quinn agreed.

Mr. Quinn took a quick shot of Lucy. "Bobby, get in the picture," he directed.

Lucy, however, was bored with posing.

She flopped down on the rug and sniffed at her shirt.

"You'd better take the costume off," Mrs. Quinn said. "We want it to be in good shape for Halloween."

Bobby started to take off Lucy's costume. She wasn't happy about it. She scampered away when Bobby tried to remove the hat. He was so busy chasing her, he barely heard the doorbell ring.

"Oh, hello, Candy," Mrs. Quinn said. "And you have Butch with you." His mother didn't sound too happy about that.

"Hi, Mrs. Q.," Candy said, stepping into the hall. "Did you know the high school is selling pumpkins in the park? They are. It's to raise money, I guess. I'm not sure what for. We thought maybe Bobby and Lucy would like to check it out. It's only two blocks away.

We could go to Shawn's and see if he wants to come with  Of course, he probably can't bring Twitch. Because Twitch is a mouse, after all—"

"Yes, I know, Candy," Mrs. Quinn said. "Why don't you come in?"

Bobby carried Lucy into the hallway. He had gotten her boots off, but she still wore her hat and shirt.

Candy stared. "Oh gosh. That's so cute. Lucy is a pirate! That's the cutest thing I ever saw. Was that your surprise?"

"Yep," Bobby answered happily.

"That's a great surprise," Candy said.

Bobby took off Lucy's hat. "Yeah, now we're both going to be pirates."

"I might be a ballerina," Candy told everyone. "Butch, would you like to be a ballerina, too?"

Butch gave himself a shake. Maybe it was his version of dancing.

Bobby put Lucy down. He took off her shirt. "I thought you were going to be a witch," he said.

"I still might be," Candy said. "Or a super-hero. Or—"

Mrs. Quinn said, "Bobby, Candy is going to the park. There's a pumpkin sale."

"Pick out a couple of pumpkins for jack-o'-lanterns," Mr. Quinn said. "I'll join you soon and help you bring them back."

Candy and Bobby and Butch and Lucy headed outside. They stopped at Shawn's house. He wasn't home, so they continued the few short blocks to the small park. Usually it was pretty quiet. Today it was full of people, noise—and pumpkins! Lots of pumpkins.

A banner made of a sheet was hung between two poles. It said, SUPPORT THE DRAGONS! BUY A PUMPKIN!

The Dragons were the high school football team.

Two big haystacks were beside the poles. On top of the haystacks sat carved jack-o'-lanterns. One was smiling. One was frowning. Each was lit up by a small flashlight inside. That made the smiling jack-o'-lantern look scary. And the frowning one even scarier!

Butch took one look, turned tail, and ran, pulling Candy along with him.

"I better follow him," Candy called.

"I don't think you have a choice," Bobby said to her back.

Lucy didn't run. She just stood and stared at the jack-o'-lanterns. For a minute, she was as still as a statue. Then she raised her nose and let out the longest howl Bobby had ever heard.

"Howwwwwwwwwwwwwwwwwl!"

This wasn't Lucy's usual howl. This was a long, creepy howl. Bobby thought a were-wolf might have a howl just like that.

Bobby gave Lucy's leash a tug. Lucy stuck her nose in the air again.

But before she began another howl, a firm voice said, "Lucy, sit!"

Bobby turned around. Lucy turned around, too. It was Coach Morris. He was Bobby's soccer coach. He was also Lucy's obedience trainer. As soon as Lucy heard Coach Morris's voice, she sat down, panting a little.

"Good dog," Coach Morris said. He gave Lucy a pat and said, "I'm glad to see she remembers me."

"Yes, sir, she does," Bobby said. Coach Morris was pretty hard to forget.

Bobby was about to look for Candy and Butch when he spotted his dad pulling Bobby's old red wagon.

"Hey, Dad," Bobby said, "is that to haul the pumpkins home in?"

"Yep," said Mr. Quinn. "Why don't I take Lucy, and you take the wagon. Get two good-size pumpkins."

"Okay," Bobby said, exchanging Lucy for the wagon. The park wasn't very large. He was sure he'd find Candy. Maybe she wanted to haul her pumpkins home in the wagon, too.

But when he spotted Candy and explained about the wagon, she shook her head. She looked glum.

"What's wrong?" Bobby asked.

"They're selling popcorn over there, so I bought some," Candy said. "I put the bag down for a minute. Butch got into it and ate it all. Popcorn is definitely not good for dogs. You know what came next."

Bobby nodded. He had seen Butch eat things he shouldn't have.

"I'm going to take him home. He's got some barfing medicine there."

Bobby pulled the wagon to the pumpkin patch and picked out two pumpkins. One was round and fat. The other was skinnier and had a curly stem. He put them in the wagon. Then he noticed several kids standing around a huge pumpkin. It was the biggest pumpkin Bobby had ever seen. The sign next to it said, POLK COUNTY'S BIGGEST PUMPKIN.

As he got closer to the pumpkin, Bobby

recognized one of the boys looking at it. His name was Jack, and he had just joined the third grade two weeks ago. He had long, shaggy brown hair that covered his ears. He kept to himself and didn't smile much.

Bobby was still shy. He didn't want to go up to the new kid and say hello. But he

remembered what it was like before he met Shawn and Candy. Before he had friends.

He walked up behind the boy. "Hi, Jack," he said.

The boy didn't bother turning around.

"Uh, hi, Jack," Bobby said a little louder.

This time Jack turned and looked at him.

"Hi," Bobby said for the third time. He could feel his face turning red.

"Hi," Jack said. But instead of staying to talk, he walked away.

Bobby frowned. He wasn't expecting that.

Then Bobby heard several long barks. It sounded like Lucy's bark. He looked around. Sure enough, there was Lucy, lying in the patch of pumpkins. Her legs were stretched out in front of her. She looked very comfortable.

Mr. Quinn was tugging on Lucy's leash. "Come on, Lucy. Get up."

Lucy gave another happy bark. She didn't move, however.

Bobby pulled the wagon over to Lucy. She looked up at him and wagged her tail.

"Lucy, up!" Bobby said in a firm voice.

He took the leash from his father's hand. Then he gave it a sharp tug. "Up!"

Lucy got up. She shook herself a little. She was ready to move on.

"How did you do that?" Mr. Quinn asked.

"I pretended I was Coach Morris," Bobby said. "He can get Lucy to do anything."

Mr. Quinn looked down at Lucy, now walking along quite contentedly. He smiled at Bobby. "It looks like you can, too."

# 4

# Pirates and Pencils

Bobby was supposed to take Lucy out in the morning before school. Sometimes he slept late. Sometimes he couldn't find his books. Most of the time, though, he and Lucy took a short walk.

Today, he smelled something good when he went downstairs. His father was drinking his coffee and his mother was frying bacon.

Lucy thought the bacon smelled good,

too. She looked hungrily at the sizzling pan.

Mrs. Quinn checked her watch. "I'll have this on the table when you get back, Bobby."

Usually, Lucy got excited when she saw her leash come out. This time she wasn't sure whether to go or to keep hoping for some bacon.

But once outside, Lucy seemed eager to enjoy the crisp fall air. She did her business, and then she and Bobby took a quick walk to the end of the block.

Mr. Davis was out picking up his newspaper.

"Hey, Bobby. Hey, Lucy," he said. "I'm glad you're here. I've got some things for you. They're right here in the front hall."

When Mr. Davis came back, he was holding a book—and something else—in his hands.

The book was *Treasure Island*. On the cover were several scary-looking pirates. One had a black beard and a wooden leg. Another had a long scar down his face. And one of them was wearing an eye patch.

"Cool!" Bobby exclaimed as he took the book.

Then Mr. Davis handed Bobby the black eye patch he'd promised him.

"Really cool!" Bobby told Mr. Davis. He hoped he'd look every bit as frightening on Halloween as these pirates.

When he got home, Bobby wolfed down his bacon and toast. Lucy had one of her fake-bacon treats. He was in a hurry to meet Shawn and tell him about the eye patch.

When they got to school, they saw Candy and their friend Dexter waiting for the bell to ring.

A boy with shaggy brown hair walked by them.

"That guy Jack is weird," Dexter said.

Bobby thought about seeing Jack at the pumpkin sale. It wasn't that long ago that Bobby hadn't talked much, either. He hadn't looked people in the eye. Maybe Jack was just shy.

"We should probably give him a chance," Bobby said.

Shawn looked at Bobby. "Probably," Shawn agreed.

"I'll give him a chance," Candy said with a shrug. "Everybody's a little weird. Some people think I talk too much."

When the bell rang, all the students hurried inside.

Room 102 was Bobby's room. It was painted bright yellow. Mrs. Lee, their

teacher, had hung up lots of posters. Some of them were about books. Some of them were about different countries. Bobby liked the room's cheerful, cluttered look.

Bobby put his jacket and backpack in his cubby. He pulled his books out of the bag. Bobby also grabbed his special pencil. It had an eraser in the shape of a bear's head. His grandparents had visited Yellowstone National Park and had sent it to him as a present.

Bobby settled into his seat. Mrs. Lee was writing on the blackboard. She was a good teacher, but Bobby liked some subjects better than others. He enjoyed reading and math. Science was usually interesting. He wasn't very good at spelling. His best subjects were art and history.

Mrs. Lee had told them at the start of

the year that she would be teaching them American history. Bobby was looking forward to learning about the pioneers. There was a real pioneer cabin in their town. The third grade would make a special visit to it in the spring.

Right now the class was studying colonial history. They were learning about the beginnings of the United States of America.

Mrs. Lee looked around the class. "You know that this semester we are going to do a lot of oral reports."

Bobby rubbed the bear head on his pencil. He wasn't as shy as he used to be. But getting up in front of the class and speaking? Ugh!

"I'm going to divide you into small groups," Mrs. Lee told the class. "I will give each group a person from colonial history.

Then you will decide how to introduce this person to our class."

Mrs. Lee put together groups of four. Bobby was happy that two of the people in his group were Shawn and Candy. The fourth student was Jack.

*Oh well,* Bobby thought. *Maybe this will be a chance to get to know him better.*

But when they were seated in a circle in a corner of the classroom, it didn't seem as if Jack was interested in getting to know them at all. He pulled a small video game from his pocket and began playing.

"What have you got there?" Candy asked.

Jack did not look up from his game.

"Cool game?" Candy tried again.

Nothing.

Shawn and Bobby looked at each other. Jack didn't seem shy. He seemed rude.

Mrs. Lee walked over to their group. She frowned a little when she saw Jack playing. She touched him on the shoulder. He looked up at her and shoved the game into his pocket.

"Your person is colonial hero Paul Revere," Mrs. Lee said.

"Paul Revere," Shawn said. "He was the one who rode his horse near Boston telling the people the British were coming."

"There's a poem about it," Candy said. "My dad read it to me when I told him we're studying colonial history. My dad's a very good reader," she informed them. "I think he wanted to be an actor. Of course, now he's a dentist—"

"That's nice, Candy," Mrs. Lee said. "I'll leave you to get started."

Bobby, Shawn, and Candy began talking about their report. They thought of different ways to introduce Paul Revere. Jack didn't say much.

"Okay," Bobby said at last. "Shawn, you'll give a report on Paul Revere's life."

"Yeah, and I'm going to dress up like him, too," Shawn said.

"I'm going to read that poem," Candy said. "I remember the beginning. 'Listen, my children, and you shall hear of the midnight ride of Paul Revere. . . .'"

She said it so loudly that all the other groups turned to look at her.

Even Jack smiled.

"I'm going to draw a picture of Paul Revere. And I'll talk about the Revolutionary War," Bobby said. Now he turned to Jack. "What are you going to do?"

Jack shrugged. "Not sure," he muttered.

Bobby, Shawn, and Candy looked at each other.

"Well, you should come up with something pretty soon," Candy said. "I mean, you wouldn't want to get a bad grade."

Jack shrugged again.

Mrs. Lee clapped her hands. "All right, children, back to your desks. Your projects will be due in one week. Each group will present them to the class."

Bobby felt his stomach twist in a little knot. At least drawing the picture would be fun.

Bobby was back at his desk when he noticed something. His pencil with the bear-head eraser was gone.

He looked around. He looked inside his desk. Then he remembered he'd had it while talking about Paul Revere.

The class was doing silent reading. Bobby went up to Mrs. Lee and asked if he could look for his pencil in the corner. She nodded.

The pencil wasn't there.

Then something caught his eye. A pencil

with a bear-head eraser. And it was sitting on Jack's desk.

Bobby walked over to Jack. He stood there nervously for a few seconds. Finally he said softly, "Jack, that pencil is mine."

Jack acted as if he didn't hear him.

Bobby put his hand on the desk. That made Jack look up.

"This is my pencil." He tried to say it a little more firmly.

Jack looked surprised. "Oh, I found it on the floor." He pushed it toward Bobby.

"Thank you," Bobby said. He went back to his desk. He took a big breath and put the pencil away.

He was sure glad that Jack hadn't argued with him about the pencil. That would have been almost as bad as not finding the pencil at all.

# Lucy at the Library

Bobby loved to draw. But he wasn't enjoying drawing today. He had finished his picture of Paul Revere on his horse. Paul Revere was easy to draw.

The horse? Not so much.

Bobby looked at the picture. His horse was too fat. Its legs were too short. It looked like a stuffed animal Bobby had when he was little. That stuffie had been through the washing machine so many times it was hard to tell just what kind of animal it was.

Lucy came prancing into the family room. She looked up at Bobby and barked. She was ready to play.

And Bobby was ready to make this picture disappear. He crumpled it into a ball and threw it on the floor.

Lucy was surprised. But she picked up the ball with her teeth. Then she dumped it on the couch next to Bobby.

Bobby shook his head. "I'm trying to get rid of it, Lucy."

He threw the paper across the room. Lucy ran after it. She didn't care if it was a bad picture. It made a good ball!

"Bobby, Shawn is here," Mrs. Quinn called from the hallway. "At least I think it's Shawn."

*What does that mean?* Bobby wondered. In a moment, he understood.

Shawn came into the room. He was wearing long socks, short pants, a white shirt, and a white wig with a small tail. He was dressed as a colonial man.

Bobby jumped off the couch. "What a great costume!"

Shawn beamed. He pointed at the pieces of his outfit. "My sister Sara's old Bermuda shorts and kneesocks. One of my

53

shirts. A vest from a suit I wore to my cous-
in's wedding."

"But the wig! How did you make that?"
Bobby asked.

"Sara helped," Shawn said. "She's good at
crafts."

Shawn pulled the wig off his head. He
showed Bobby how the cotton balls were
glued together and attached to a small beanie-
like cap.

"Cool," Bobby said.

"I'm going to wear it for our report. And
I decided I'm going to wear it for Halloween, too," Shawn told him. He placed the
wig on the coffee table.

"How's your report coming?" Bobby asked.

"Pretty good. I'm almost done," Shawn
said. "What about you?"

Bobby shook his head. "I can't get Paul

54

Revere's horse right." He found the balled-up picture and smoothed it out so Shawn could see it. He liked drawing, too.

"Horses are hard to draw," Shawn said. "You know, I took a book out of the library that showed how to draw all kinds of animals. I don't remember the name, but just ask the librarian. She knows everything."

Bobby perked up. "That's a good idea!"

At dinner, Bobby said, "There's a book I need at the library. It's about drawing animals." He explained about Paul Revere's horse.

"We can go tonight," Mr. Quinn said.

"It will be a good walk for Lucy," Mrs. Quinn added.

It was a dark, chilly night. Bobby was glad that the library was only a few blocks away.

"Look, Dad," Bobby said. "Some people

have already decorated their houses for Halloween."

Mr. Quinn nodded. "A couple of our neighbors have gone all out."

Bobby pointed to a brick house across the street. On the porch, next to a carved pumpkin, was a ghost made from a sheet attached to a pole. It was bigger than Bobby. Every so often, it said, "Boo!"

Lucy was interested in that ghost. She tugged Bobby toward it. He didn't mind. He wanted to see it, too.

When they got closer to the porch, Lucy ran up the stairs. Just then, the ghost let out a loud "Boo!"

Lucy jumped! She ran down the stairs much faster than she had gone up. Now she pulled Bobby away from the brick house, trotting quickly along.

By the time they arrived at the library, she was panting hard.

"I'm going to mail some letters at the post office," Mr. Quinn said. "Be as quick as you can."

Bobby nodded. He hurried inside the library and headed to the Children's Room. He liked it there. A small fireplace ringed by several comfortable chairs made it a good place to read. But he didn't have time for that tonight.

He knew he should ask the librarian for help finding the book he needed. He couldn't. He felt too shy.

Maybe the librarian knew how he was feeling. She came over to him and asked, "Are you looking for something special?"

Bobby nodded. "A book on drawing horses," he said quietly.

The young librarian smiled at him. "I think I know just which book you mean."

She walked over to the shelves and found the drawing books. She pulled out one called *The Art of the Horse*. Then she found another, *Simple Ways to Draw Animals*.

"These might help," the librarian said.

"Absolutely!" Bobby agreed.

He took his books to the checkout desk.

He was so busy looking through the pages he didn't notice the boy in line in front of him.

Then he saw that the boy had long hair. He was checking out books about Paul Revere.

Bobby caught up to Jack on the way to the door. He tapped him on the shoulder.

Jack looked around. When he saw it was Bobby, he nodded.

Bobby pointed to Jack's books. "Have you decided what your report will be about?"

Jack said, "I'm going to talk about Paul Revere when he was a silversmith. My mom has a Paul Revere silver cup. I'm going to bring it in."

"A real one?" Bobby asked, his eyes wide.

Jack shook his head. "She got it at a gift shop in Boston. It's a copy of a cup he made."

Bobby nodded. "Sounds good," he said. He hoped his horse would work out as well.

Mr. Quinn was waiting with Lucy when they got outside. Bobby wasn't very good at introducing people. He waved goodbye to Jack.

Lucy liked meeting new people. She ran toward Jack and blocked him from leaving.

Jack leaned over and patted Lucy.

"Hello," Mr. Quinn said. "I'm Bobby's dad. And this is Lucy."

"I have a dog, too. His name is Prince." Jack spotted a red car. "There's my mom. I gotta go."

"I didn't catch that boy's name," Mr. Quinn said as they headed for home.

"It's Jack. He's new," Bobby replied.

"Do you like him?" Mr. Quinn asked.

Bobby thought about that question. Jack had seemed a little friendlier tonight. But did Bobby like him?

He wasn't sure.

# 6

# Show-and-Tell

"**M**om, it's show-and-tell today," Bobby said.

He gulped down his milk and shoved a piece of toast in his mouth. There hadn't been time to walk Lucy. And if he didn't find something right away to bring to school, he was going to be late.

Mrs. Quinn frowned. "Why did you leave this until the last minute?"

Bobby jumped out of his seat. "Sorry, I forgot."

"Shawn will be here anytime now," his mother informed him.

Bobby ran up to his room. He'd find something in there he could use.

Lucy ran right behind him. Usually running went on outside. Running indoors was a treat.

Looking around his room, Bobby tried to figure out what to bring.

His soccer ball? Too big.

His lucky penny? Too small.

The postcard his cousins had sent him from their vacation in California? Too boring.

A photograph on his dresser caught Bobby's eye. His dad had printed some of the photos he had taken on his phone. One

of them was the picture of Lucy in her pirate costume.

The class could have a sneak peek at Lucy in her costume!

Then he had another good idea. A great idea! He could bring Lucy's costume so everyone could see it close up.

Bobby grabbed the photo and bounded downstairs. Lucy bounded after him.

"Mom," he said, a little out of breath. "I've got this picture of Lucy as a pirate." He waved it in the air.

"Oh, that will be good," she said, looking at the clock.

"And I want to take Lucy's costume to school, too," Bobby added.

Mrs. Quinn shook her head. "It might get dirty, Bobby."

"I'll be really careful," Bobby pleaded.

"I'm not even sure where it is," said his mother.

"It's in the hall closet," Bobby told her. "I saw it there yesterday."

The doorbell rang. Mrs. Quinn opened the door.

"Hi, Mrs. Quinn," Shawn said.

"Bobby is almost ready," she answered. She looked around to make sure that was true.

Bobby hurried into his jacket and pulled his backpack out of the closet. He also took out Lucy's costume, still in its Pet-O-Rama bag. "Mom, please? It would be so cool."

"All right, take it," Mrs. Quinn said. "But leave the boots. They'd be easy to lose."

Bobby grabbed the boots out of the bag and handed them to his mother. The T-shirt and the hat were on the little plastic hanger. He could just hold it up during show-and-tell.

"Be careful with it," his mother reminded him.

"I will!" Bobby yelled as he rushed out the door. "Thanks, Mom."

The boys had to practically run to beat the school bell. They didn't have much time to talk.

Bobby held up the bag from Pet-O-Rama. "Show-and-tell," he gasped as they raced toward school. "Lucy's pirate costume."

"Awesome," Shawn said. "All I came up with was a video game. And it's not even new."

Bobby and Shawn got to their room just as the bell was ringing. Bobby put the costume in his cubby with his jacket. Show-and-tell wasn't until the afternoon.

Bobby figured Mrs. Lee thought the class had most of its brainpower in the morning. That's when she taught the harder subjects, anyway.

After lunch, Bobby laid out the photograph and the bag with Lucy's costume on his desk.

Jack was walking by. He stopped to look at the picture.

"That's your dog, Lucy," Jack said.

Bobby tried to be friendly. "Yes, she's going to be a pirate for Halloween." He took the costume out of the bag. "Here's her costume."

Jack picked it up and looked at it. "Nice. Prince is about Lucy's size. He would look good in a costume like this."

He put down the pirate outfit. But he took another glance back at it as he walked to his seat.

Bobby was glad Jack liked the costume. Still, he hoped that Jack wasn't going to buy Prince a pirate costume. He wanted Lucy to be the only dog wearing that costume on Halloween.

Later in the afternoon, Mrs. Lee clapped her hands. "Time for show-and-tell. I know you have interesting things to share."

Bobby enjoyed show-and-tell. Sometimes kids brought really neat stuff. Last week, Dexter had brought his grandfather's ball made of gum wrappers. It had taken years to collect the wrappers and weave them together. And it wasn't the size of a baseball. It was the size of a beach ball.

Today, Marta was first up. She had brought the electric pan her mother used to make tortillas. It was one of the family's favorite foods. The machine looked a little like a waffle iron. Marta explained how her mother made the tortilla mix and put it in the pan. Then Marta took a tortilla out of a little brown bag and showed it to the class.

"You can wrap it around all kinds of food," Marta told them.

Bobby wished Marta could have done an eat-and-tell. A tortilla would taste good about now.

Candy was up next. To Bobby's surprise, for once she didn't have much to say.

She went to the front of the class and held up a stuffed sock monkey. "My mom said I should bring this," Candy began. "She said it shows how you can recycle things like old socks. She made this for me when I was little."

Candy made a face at the monkey. "I never really liked it. It kind of scared me."

And with that, she sat down.

Mrs. Lee looked around the class. "Bobby, how about you?"

Bobby felt a few butterflies in his stom-ach. But he was eager to show the class Lucy's pirate costume.

"I'm going to be a pirate for Hallow-een and so is my dog, Lucy," Bobby said in a voice he hoped was loud enough for the class to hear.

Before he could say one more word, a loud ringing broke into the room.

This wasn't the regular bell. This was the fire-alarm bell. Once before when Bobby had to speak in class, the fire alarm had rung. Then he had been happy. Now he wasn't. He had wanted to show Room 102 Lucy's costume.

Mrs. Lee stood up. "Class, this is a fire drill. Move quickly and quietly. Then line up."

Bobby shoved Lucy's picture and the

costume in the bag. He grabbed his jacket and tossed the bag into his cubby. Mrs. Lee's class was out the door in no time flat.

He heard the librarian whisper to Mrs. Lee, "It's such a strange time for a fire drill. We never have one this late in the afternoon."

That made Bobby wonder. *Could this be a real fire?* He looked around, but he didn't see any flames. He sniffed. No smoke. At least none that he could smell.

As soon as he was outside, he did hear something. The wail of the fire engine. *Uh-oh!*

Room 102 went to their assigned spot outside the school.

"Line up, children," Mrs. Lee said. "I'm going to do a head count."

All the heads were watching the fire

73

engine that had just pulled up to the curb.
Several firefighters in full gear piled out and
rushed into the school.

Candy was right behind Bobby. "This is
kind of scary," she said. "I don't want to see

any flames shooting out the window. I don't want my stuff to get burned. Even that stupid sock monkey."

"I still don't see anything that looks like fire," Bobby whispered to her.

What he did see was the principal, Ms. Alma V. Ross, standing on the steps of the school. She paced back and forth for a few moments. Then a fireman came out of the building. He talked to Ms. Ross, who nodded.

"Children," Ms. Ross said in her loudest voice, "this was a false alarm."

"Oh, good," Candy said with a sigh.

"The firefighters are double-checking to make sure everything is safe. When they are done, you can return to your classrooms."

It took a while longer, but finally, a fireman came out and gave everyone the thumbs-up sign.

Ms. Ross said, "Thank you. Students, let's all give our fire department a round of applause, shall we?"

After the applause, the kids headed back to their rooms. The getting back was not nearly as orderly as the going out had been.

Finally the third-graders were in their seats again.

Mrs. Lee looked at the clock. "Oh dear. The dismissal bell is going to ring soon. Let's spend the last few minutes clearing our spaces."

Bobby put his books in his desk. Then he looked around for the bag with Lucy's costume and his photo.

What had he done with it? He tried to remember.

The bell rang. Bobby made his way to his cubby. He had tossed the bag in there, hadn't he? But when he looked inside, all he saw were a couple of books, a pair of gym shoes, and an old lunch sack.

Lucy's costume was gone.

# 7

# Lucy Sniffs Around

Bobby worried all the way home about telling his mother Lucy's costume was missing. He thought she would be mad. After all, she hadn't wanted him to take it in the first place.

But when he told her the story, she put her arm around him. "Let's get you some milk and cookies," she said. "It sounds like you had a rough day."

"I'm pretty sure I put it in my cubby before we left during the fire alarm," Bobby told her. He took a couple of cookies from the red jar on the kitchen counter.

Mrs. Quinn brought over a glass of milk. "You looked there?"

Bobby nodded. "I told Mrs. Lee. She helped me look around. It wasn't in the cubby, and it wasn't on the floor. She said we could look more tomorrow. She'll ask if anyone saw the bag."

"Maybe someone saw it and kept it for you on their way out during the alarm," Mrs. Quinn said. "I'm sure no one took it on purpose."

Bobby put his head down and ate his cookies. He certainly didn't want to think that anyone had taken Lucy's costume on purpose.

On the way home, Bobby had remembered what Jack had said about his own dog looking cute in a pirate costume. That wasn't proof of anything, of course.

The pencil with the bear-head eraser? Jack certainly could have found it on the floor.

And the fact that Jack wasn't friendly didn't mean anything, either. Bobby was sure that plenty of kids had pegged *him* as unfriendly when he was only shy.

"Bobby," his mother asked, looking at him carefully, "you don't think someone took it, do you?"

Bobby shook his head. "Nope."

That night at dinner, Mr. Quinn had an idea about what to do next.

"Why don't we let Lucy sniff around the classroom?" he asked. "She loved burying her nose in that costume. And beagles are known for being able to find things."

Bobby looked back and forth between his dad and his mom. He was pretty sure his mother wouldn't agree.

To his surprise, however, Mrs. Quinn nodded. "I think that's a great idea! I'll call Ms. Ross tomorrow and see if I can bring Lucy to school at lunchtime."

Lucy heard her name. She padded over from her dog dish, where she was eating her own dinner. She hopped up on the empty fourth chair at the table and wagged her tail. It was almost as if she knew she was going to school. And she liked the idea!

Everyone laughed.

"It's not just for a visit, though, Lucy," Bobby said. "I hope you can find your costume."

The next morning, first thing, Bobby went up to Mrs. Lee, who was writing on the board.

"Mrs. Lee, will you remember to ask the class about Lucy's pirate costume?" he asked.

Mrs. Lee turned to him. "Yes, of course. Ms. Ross told me we're going to get a visitor at lunch today if the costume isn't found by then."

Bobby nodded.

"Well, maybe we can save your mother and Lucy a trip," she said.

As soon as the class was in their seats, Mrs. Lee explained about the lost bag.

"Has anyone seen it?" she asked.

No one raised a hand.

Bobby turned to look at Jack. But Jack was not at his desk.

A few moments later, when Mrs. Lee took

the roll call, she did not seem surprised Jack was absent. She didn't even call his name.

Halfway into math class, a folded-up piece of paper landed on Bobby's desk.

Surprised, he opened it. It was a note from Candy. It said, *Shawn told me LUCY is coming to school. True or false?* Candy had drawn a little picture of Lucy at the bottom of the page. At least Bobby thought it was supposed to be Lucy.

Bobby nodded nervously at Candy. He didn't want Mrs. Lee to think he wasn't paying attention.

It wasn't until they got to the lunchroom that Bobby explained.

"I don't think you'll get to see Lucy," he said.

"Why not?" Candy asked. "I've never seen a dog in school. That would be funny."

"Lucy's coming here to work, not to play," Shawn told her before taking a bite of his sandwich.

Candy circled the straw in her juice.

"You're lucky. Lucy can work and play. I'd be happy if Butch would just sleep less."

"Have you decided if you're going to dress Butch up for Halloween?" Shawn asked.

"I'm not taking him out with us," said Candy. "My mom's afraid he'll get into the treats. Candy gives him gas." She clapped her hand over her mouth. Then she said, "I didn't mean me, Candy, gives him gas. . . ."

Bobby and Shawn were laughing. Bobby managed to say, "We know what you meant."

Mrs. Lee came up to their table. "Bobby, your mother is here. And Lucy, of course. Let's see if we can find that costume."

When he got to Room 102, Bobby had to agree with Candy. It was funny—and fun—to see a dog at school.

Lucy certainly understood she was some-place new. She was standing very straight.

She looked around, her head held high.

She didn't jump on Bobby like she usually did when she saw him. She padded over to him and licked his hand as he leaned down to pet her. Then she started sniffing the carpet. Lucy seemed to know she was there to do a job.

Mrs. Quinn pulled a small black boot from Lucy's pirate costume out of her coat pocket.

"I thought I would let Lucy smell the boot. I hope she gets the idea to find the costume," she explained.

Mrs. Lee smiled. "Well, that's the way it works in movies. Let's see if it works in Room 102."

Mrs. Quinn gave the boot to Bobby. "You try," she said.

Bobby had barely leaned down with the

boot in his hand when Lucy began prancing. She inhaled the boot's smell. She seemed happy to just keep doing that.

Bobby looked at his mother.

"Okay, take the boot away," she told him.

Bobby shoved the boot into his pocket. Lucy looked around, confused. For a minute, it didn't seem as if anything else would happen.

But as Mrs. Quinn led Lucy around the room, she seemed to get the idea.

She sniffed at desks. She smelled along the walls.

"Take her over to the cubbies," Mrs. Lee suggested.

That was a good idea.

Lucy became excited as soon as she got close to the wall with the brightly colored cubbies. She stood up and put her front

paws against the lowest cubbies. She gave a little howl.

"I don't get it," Bobby said. "We looked in my cubby about three times."

Mrs. Quinn took Lucy in her arms. Now that she was higher, Lucy became more excited. Her nose quivered. But it wasn't Bobby's cubby that interested her. She tried to claw and wiggle her way up to the cubby above.

"There's nothing in that one," Mrs. Lee said. "It's too high for the kids to reach."

Lucy still pushed her nose in that direction.

Mrs. Lee stuck her hand into the cubby and felt around. "It seems empty."

Mrs. Quinn was taller than Mrs. Lee. She reached her hand to the back of the cubby. "I think I found some buried treasure," she said happily. She pulled out the bag with the pirate costume.

When Bobby saw it, he was thrilled—and relieved.

"How did it get up there?" a puzzled Mrs. Lee asked.

"I tossed it up to my cubby on my way out during the fire alarm. Maybe I threw it too high," Bobby said. Then he had another thought. "Or maybe it didn't make the cubby at all, and one of the firefighters or the janitor picked it up from the floor and stuck it in there."

Meanwhile, Lucy couldn't wait to get to the bag in Mrs. Quinn's hand. She wiggled around. *Let me at it!*

Everyone laughed.

"Well, Lucy, looks like you're going to be ready for Halloween after all," Mrs. Lee said.

"I don't even know if Lucy should dress up as a pirate," Bobby said.

"Why not?" Mrs. Quinn asked. "After all this trouble?"

Bobby smiled. "She ought to go as a detective!"

# 8

# *Howl-loween*

Lucy was gone by the time Room 102 came back from lunch.

"Did Lucy find the costume?" Candy asked as she went to her seat.

Bobby smiled.

"Class, I'd like your attention, please," Mrs. Lee said. She leaned forward in her chair. "Some of you may have noticed that Jack is not here today."

A few of the kids nodded.

"He is absent because he's getting fitted for a new hearing aid. Jack had hearing problems before, so he was tested when he came to our school. It turns out his old aid wasn't working very well."

Bobby remembered the times when it seemed as if Jack wasn't paying attention to him. Maybe it was because Jack couldn't hear him clearly.

"Tomorrow," Mrs. Lee went on, "when Jack returns, he might want to talk about his new hearing aid, and he might not. Let him take the lead. Just treat Jack the way you would want to be treated." She smiled at the class. "That's what we should always try to do in Room 102. Do you have any questions?"

Marta raised her hand. "Will we be able to see Jack's hearing aid?" she asked.

"I don't know," Mrs. Lee answered. "I guess we'll find out tomorrow."

"My aunt got a hearing aid, and she said it made her life a whole lot easier," Dexter commented.

"I imagine the same will be true for Jack," Mrs. Lee told them.

Bobby figured Jack wouldn't want to say anything about a new hearing aid. Bobby knew he wouldn't if it were him.

Bobby turned out to be wrong. The next day, when Jack came to class, it was easy to see he wasn't ashamed of his hearing aid. It was bright blue!

Before the bell rang, Bobby watched Mrs. Lee talking to Jack. Bobby saw him nodding.

When everyone was settled, Mrs. Lee said, "We're going to change our schedule today. Let's continue our show-and-tell that got interrupted by the fire alarm."

Mrs. Lee smiled at Jack. "I think Jack has something he would like to share with us."

A happy Jack marched to the front of the room.

"So, I guess Mrs. Lee told you I just got a new hearing aid," Jack began. "I was having trouble hearing unless it was really quiet or the person was speaking clearly. Yesterday, I got to take my new hearing aid home."

Jack's hair still covered his ears. He pushed it back on one side so everyone could see. "The doctor asked me whether I wanted one that was skin color or something flashier." Jack grinned. "I picked flashy."

A blue band was fitted around Jack's ear. "Another part of the hearing aid is inside my ear," Jack went on. "It's going to be good to really hear what's going on from now on."

Jack sat down. Everybody clapped.

Now Bobby was happier than ever that he hadn't said anything about Jack taking Lucy's costume. You couldn't accuse some-

one without real proof. He had learned that lesson for sure.

Later that afternoon, the history groups met to talk about their projects. They were due the next day!

"My report is done. So is my picture of Paul Revere," Bobby said. "I'd like to work more on the horse. But it's better than when I started."

"I memorized part of my poem, and I'll read the rest," Candy said. "Do you want to hear it?"

"Uh, we can hear it tomorrow," Bobby said politely.

"I'm ready to talk about Paul Revere, the silversmith," Jack said.

"And I'll be in my costume to talk about Paul Revere's life," Shawn said. Then he added, "Hey, I'm lucky."

"Why's that?" Bobby asked.

"Tomorrow's Halloween! I'll only have to change my clothes once!"

Sure enough, the group gave their reports in the morning, but Shawn got to stay in his Paul Revere outfit all afternoon. Everyone else put on their costumes before last period.

"Arrgh, matey! Walk the plank," Bobby said to Candy once he had his pirate costume on, complete with the eye patch.

"Well, if I do, I won't get wet." Candy had been so impressed with the firefighters during the alarm, she decided to dress up as one. She wore a red plastic raincoat with a thick black belt, a red plastic firefighter's hat, and black boots. A length of rubber hose was curled up in her coat pocket.

Bobby looked around the class. There

were some pretty good costumes. Dexter was Spider-Man. Marta was a flower with colorful petals attached to her headband. Jack was a baseball player in a blue uniform that matched his hearing aid.

Finally it was time for the parade to begin. All the classes would march around the school. They'd get to see each other's costumes. Parents, grandparents, friends, and neighbors came to watch the parade, too.

Bobby was happy the day was sunny and not too cold. Having to wear a coat over a Halloween costume was the worst!

"I know everyone is excited," Mrs. Lee said with a smile. "But let's try to stay in line as we march."

Lots of people were waiting outside. It seemed as if half the town had come to watch the Halloween parade.

Bobby saw Mr. Davis standing with Shawn's dad at the edge of the playground. He gave them both a big wave.

Then Bobby heard a very familiar bark. He knew what that meant! Sure enough, he turned his head and saw Lucy with his mother.

Lucy looked great! She was dressed in her pirate costume. Her shirt was on. Her boots were on. The pirate hat was atop her head.

Some of the students saw Lucy in her costume. They nudged each other and pointed her out. Lucy sat up straighter.

Then Lucy spotted Bobby. Mrs. Quinn held her leash tight. Lucy wanted to join that parade.

"Later, Lucy," Bobby called to her. "We'll all go trick-or-treating. You, me, Shawn, and Candy."

Bobby noticed Jack right behind him. "Do you want to come with us, too?" he asked.

Jack smiled. "Sure."

Lucy chose that moment to give a long howl. If you listened closely, it sounded like *Haaallooweeen!*

"That's right, Lucy," Bobby said. "Happy Haaallooweeen!"

# Read all the books
# about Bobby and Lucy!

# Absolutely Lucy

Bobby's mother smiled. "Now it's time for your special present," she said.

His father said, "Close your eyes."

Bobby was glad to close his eyes. It would be easier to look surprised when he opened them.

"Okay, Bobby," his father called, "you can look!"

Bobby opened his eyes. He didn't have to pretend to be surprised. Or happy. In his father's arms was a puppy. The cutest, squirmiest little dog Bobby had ever seen.

# Lucy on the Loose

"Ben!" Shawn said. "What happened to Lucy?"

"She . . . she ran away!" Ben said in a shaky voice.

Bobby jumped up. "Ran away? Where?"

"That way." Ben was confused. He pointed in one direction. "Or maybe that way." He pointed in the other direction.

"Which way was it?" Shawn demanded.

"I'm not sure." Ben was almost crying. "But she was chasing a big orange C-A-T!"

# Look at Lucy!

On the way out, a large, colorful poster taller than the boys caught Bobby's eye.

The poster had a drawing of different kinds of animals crowded together in front of a television camera. Across the top were the words WANTED: SPOKESPET FOR PET-O-RAMA! Under the picture of the animals it said, "Is your pet cute? Smart? Funny? Enter the Pet-O-Rama spokespet contest and your pet could be on TV!"

Bobby read the poster carefully. Cute, smart, funny? That described Lucy! She could win the spokespet contest, easy!